A DECISION IS YOURS BOOK

Finders, Keepers?

BY ELIZABETH CRARY

ILLUSTRATED BY REBEKAH STRECKER

LC 87-60369
ISBN 0-943990-38-6 Paper
ISBN 0-943990-39-4 Library Binding

Published by

Parenting Press, Inc.
P.O. Box 75267
Seattle, WA 98125

BEFORE YOU BEGIN

Most books you read tell you about other people's decisions.

This book is different! **You** make the decisions. You decide what happens next.

Have you ever done something that turned out terribly? Have you ever wished you had a chance to go back and see what would happen if you did something differently? This book gives you that chance.

In this book, you and your friend Jerry find a wallet with some money in it. You must decide what to do with the wallet. You make the decisions.

Turn the page and see what happens.

Have you ever found something you really 1
wanted to keep? Maybe a watch with a calculator, or a shiny bracelet, or some money? After all "finders, keepers; losers, weepers," right? Soon you will find something!

You and your friend Jerry are at the swimming pool in the park near your house. It is a hot day and you have been swimming. You are tired and have decided to go to Jerry's house.

Jerry is a lot of fun. He has the biggest collection of computer games you have ever seen. This morning he said he has a new game and you want to try it.

You and Jerry walk across the park toward Jerry's house. The sun is really bright. You can feel the heat on your back. You flop down on the ground in the shade of a tree. "What I want right now is a cool ice cream cone," you say.

Jerry flops down beside you. "That's a great idea. How much money do you have?"

Turn to page 3.

2

You check your pocket. A quarter, a dime, and two nickels. "Forty-five cents. Not enough for a cone."

Jerry counts his money. "No good, I only have seventeen cents."

You sit there wishing you could buy an ice cream cone. Suddenly, you see something on the grass beside the path. As you race over, you notice it looks like a wallet.

Your friend says, "Hey, look at this. I wonder who it belongs to." And he starts to open the wallet.

"No! Don't do that," you say. "It's not yours. Let's turn it in to the Lost and Found at the pool."

Jerry says, "What's the matter? Are you chicken? Come on. Let's just look. I'm not going to take anything. I just want to see how much money there is."

If you decide to give it to the Lost and Found, turn to page 7.

If you decide to just look at the money, turn to page 11.

4

Jerry takes his foot off the wallet and bends over to pick it up. You grab it before he does. 5

"I'm going to return it. Are you coming?" you ask Jerry.

"Chicken, chicken. You are a chicken!" Jerry taunts.

"That's right!" you reply. "Better a live chicken than a dead duck. And that's what I'll be if my dad finds out I took the money."

"Aw, come on, Tyrone," Jerry says. "Your dad won't find out."

"You don't know my dad," you reply gloomily. "He finds out about everything."

Turn to page 36.

6

You ask Jerry to give you the wallet so you can take it to the pool. He says, "No!" You grab for the wallet and knock it from his hand.

Before you can pick up the wallet, Jerry is standing with one foot on it. He flaps his arms like a bird and chants, "Chicken, chicken! You are a chicken! You are a chicken!"

You are not sure what to do. Jerry says, "Come on, it won't hurt you to look. I'm not going to take anything."

If you decide to give it to the Lost and Found, turn to page 5.

If you are curious to see if there is any money, turn to page 9.

8

Jerry picks up the wallet and pulls all the bills out. "Boy, look at all that money. Mr. French must be really rich. If I had that much money, I would buy a new game for the computer. What would you buy?"

"Maybe something for my bike," you reply. "Like a basket or a tire pump. How rich do you think Mr. French is?"

"I don't know, but rich enough he won't miss this. And that is for sure."

"I'm not so sure. Maybe he is rich *because* he keeps track of his money all the time."

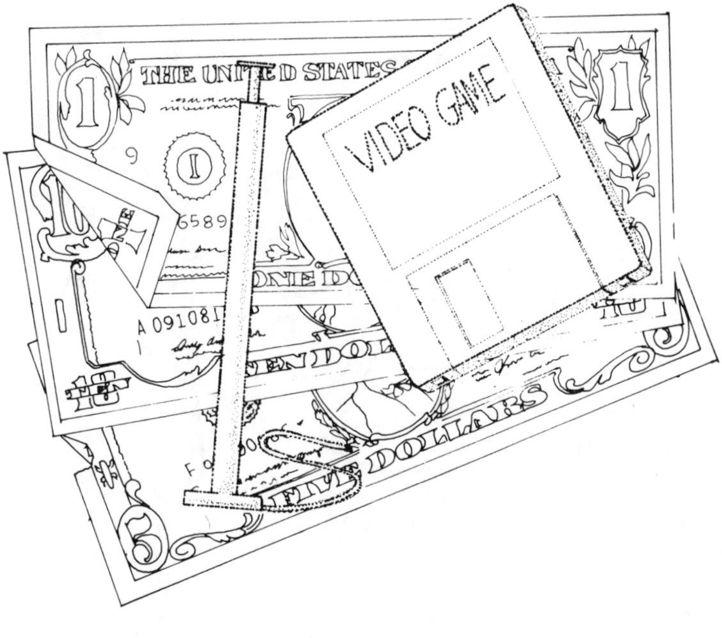

Turn to page 14.

10

Jerry opens the wallet. It belongs to a Mr. French. He lives nearby.

He looks in the bill compartment. "Wow! Look at all that money." He counts it. "Ten, twenty, thirty, forty, one, two, three, four. Wow! What I could do with $44," Jerry says.

You say, "But that's not right. It's not yours."

"Aw, he won't miss a dollar or two," Jerry replies. "And just think how nice an ice cream cone would be. Cool and creamy. It would taste mmm-mmm good."

If you decide he really won't miss $2.00,
turn to page 25.

If you decide not to take the money,
turn to page 18.

12

You decide not to leave either your name or your phone number.

You walk out with Jerry and climb a tree out front. While you climb he complains that you are a coward.

"Look, bug off! I did what I thought was right," you say. "There is nothing you can do now unless you want to want to go back and get the wallet."

Just then a man comes up. "I'm Mr. French. Are you the two kids who turned in my wallet?"

You nod. "Well, I want to give you a reward for turning it in. May I give you each a dollar?" You both nod and he says, "You acted honestly, and saved me a lot of worry. Thank you."

The End

14 Jerry spreads the bills out in his hands and stares at them. "I know what we could do. We can take all the money and turn in the wallet. We can tell them there was no money when we found it."

"But Jerry," you reply, shocked, "that's stealing. You could be arrested for that."

"Don't be a scaredy cat. No one arrests kids."

"Yes, they do. I heard of two kids arrested for shoplifting. They had to go to the police station and call their parents from there."

"Oh, come on, Tyrone. No one will know," he says.

"Yes, they will. I am not going to risk it."

"What do you want to do then, leave the wallet here?" he asks.

If you take it to the clerk, turn to page 52.

If you leave it there, turn to page 17.

16

17

You put the wallet on the grass where Jerry found it. Both of you start off toward your house again.

Somehow it doesn't seem right to leave it there. You argue with yourself each step. "If I lost my wallet, I would like someone to turn it in, but I am too tired to walk back up there again."

Finally you decide you have to go back. You tell Jerry, "I'm going to turn the wallet in to the Lost and Found. You can come if you want to. I'll be as fast as I can."

You pick up the wallet and run to the clerk before Jerry can change your mind. The clerk thanks you for turning the wallet in and you both head for home.

The End

18 "Come on, Jerry. That's stealing. My parents would be *so* mad."

"Okay, scaredy cat," he replies, "wait till I tell the others you're nothing but a big chicken. An ice cream cone would be real nice."

"You don't know my dad. He would be *real* mad."

Turn to page 39.

NIKE

You are scared and run out of the store.

The clerk yells, "Stop that boy!" A woman coming in grabs hold of you. You try to squirm free, but she is holding you too tightly. She brings you back in.

The clerk tells her, "I think this kid stole someone's wallet." Then he turns to you and says, "Tyrone, do you want to give me the wallet or shall I take it?"

You give him the wallet. "Here it is, but I didn't steal it. I found it. I was going to give it back. Honest!"

The clerk looks skeptical. "You are in trouble. You can call Mr. French and tell him what you have done, or I will call the police. Which is it?"

You decide to call Mr. French.

Turn to page 22.

22 The clerk takes you to the phone and dials Mr. French's number. While you wait for him to answer, you think about what you will say.

When he answers, you tell him, "My name is Tyrone. I have your wallet, and my friend and I used some money. But I will pay it back when I get my allowance tomorrow."

"Thank you for calling me and telling me you found my wallet, Tyrone. How much money did you spend?"

"Only 95 cents for an ice cream cone. And I will pay you back," you assure him. "Jerry spent 95 cents, too."

"Where can I get my wallet today?" he asks." And when will you pay me back?"

"I'll leave the wallet at the 7th Heaven Ice Cream Shop, and bring you your money by noon tomorrow."

"Okay, Tyrone. And thank you again for calling me."

"Whew, I'm glad that is over!" you say to yourself.

The End

24

You try to convince yourself Mr. French has lots of money. He won't even miss two dollars.

Jerry takes out two dollars and gives you one. Then he tries to put the wallet in his pocket but it is too big. "You carry it," he says, giving you the wallet.

"I don't want it," you say.

"What do you want me to do with it? Hang it around my neck so everyone can see it?" he asks in an irritated tone.

"Okay," you reply and slowly slip the wallet into your pocket. Jerry is a lot of fun and you would like to be with him, but....

"Jerry," you say, "I really don't think we should take the money."

"Don't be silly. We aren't stealing the money. We will borrow it and return it later."

If you decide to borrow the money for the ice cream cone, turn to page 45.

If you decide it is not right to borrow the money, turn to page 41.

26

The clerk looks at the wallet and says, "This belongs to Mr. French, not you. I want you to phone him and tell him you have his wallet.

You are really scared. You think about what to do.

If you agree to call Mr. French, turn to page 22.

If you are too scared to call, turn to page 29.

You open your mouth to explain that Jerry made you take the wallet. All that comes out is "I-I-I-I...." Suddenly you panic and run for the door.

As you reach the door, it opens and a police officer comes in. The clerk yells, "Grab that boy. I think he stole a wallet."

The officer grabs you. You can't wriggle free. "Now, young man, what is this all about?" he asks.

"Well, sir," you explain, "Jerry and I found the wallet. Jerry made me take the money and buy an ice cream cone. He said he would tell the clerk I took the money if I didn't come."

"First, you are always responsible for what you do. Jerry didn't make you come unless he dragged you. Did he drag you?" You shake your head no. "You could have told the clerk instead of ordering a cone. You knew it was wrong."

The officer says, "You may call Mr. French and explain what you did or I will take you to the police station and call your dad. Your choice."

You call Mr. French. He is glad to know where his wallet is. He says he will pick it up later this afternoon. The officer says you can go. As you go, you think, "I'm glad Dad didn't have to come to the police station to get me."

The End

Pool Rules
1
2
3
4
5

"You want to change your mind?" Jerry asks.

"NO!" you reply firmly.

"All right! You'll be sorry," he says, and starts towards the building.

You go along, too. When he finds the clerk, he tells her that he found the wallet and wants to turn it in. Then he adds with a mean grin, "Most of the money is there, but my friend took some and wouldn't give it back."

"Is that true?" asks the clerk.

"No," you answer. "See, my pockets are empty. Ask him to empty his pockets and you will find two dollars *he* took from the wallet."

"Liar," he says. "The money is mine. I earned it."

"Well," says the clerk, "My guess is that one of you took some money. I will step in the back for one minute. When I come back ...

Turn to page 33.

32

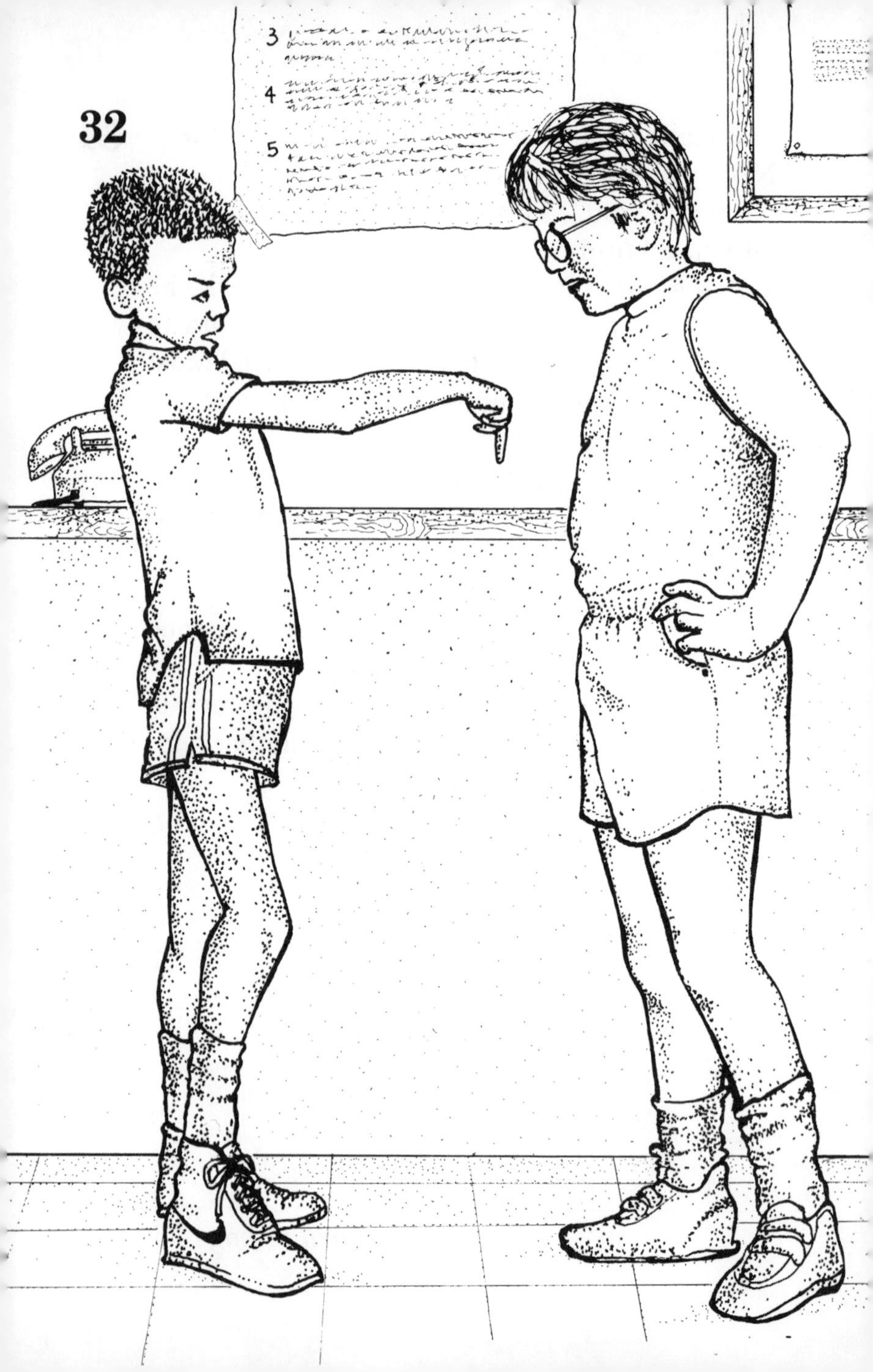

"... I expect to see the money on the counter. If the money is on the counter, I will not do anything else. If not, I will turn *both* of your names over to Mr. French. And he can call the police if he wishes. Is that clear?"

As soon as she leaves you say, "Jerry, please put the money up or we will *both* get in big trouble."

"Oh, all right, if you insist," he says as he pulls the money out and puts it on the counter.

The clerk comes back, sees the money and says, "Wise decision. Now scram, and I will phone Mr. French."

The End

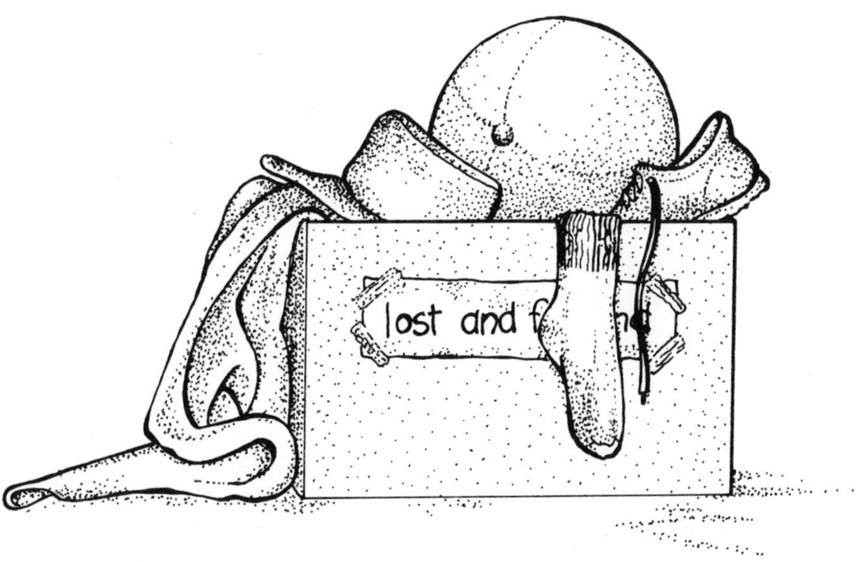

34 You decide you really can't borrow the money for the ice cream cones from the wallet. "Look, Jerry," you say, "I can't do it. Give me back the money, and we can call Mr. French."

"Heck NO! You keep the wallet. I want the ice cream cone," shouts Jerry. Then he stomps off into the shop.

"Great going," you say to yourself. "Now I have the wallet, no cone, and Jerry's mad at me. What do I do now?"

"I could go in after Jerry, but he might still be mad. I could phone Mr. French and tell him where his wallet is. But Jerry would be mad for sure. Or I could wait and I might get caught with the wallet. Ugh! What a mess."

You wish you could give the wallet back to Jerry.

Turn to page 56.

"I'm going to turn the wallet in. You can come if you want to," you tell Jerry and you grab the wallet from him.

Jerry follows you and grumbles the whole time.

You go to the clerk and say, "I found this wallet on the grass beside the gravel path."

The clerk asks, "Would you like to leave your name so the owner can thank you?"

If you decide to leave your name, turn to page 59.

If you decide not to leave your name, turn to page 13.

37

You reach for the wallet to take it to the Lost and Found at the pool. But Jerry grabs it before you do.

Jerry opens the wallet, takes a dollar out and puts it in his pocket. Then he hands you a dollar.

"No! I won't take it. That's stealing!" You tell him. "And if you have any sense, you will put the money back and give the wallet to the clerk."

"No way. Finders, keepers; losers, weepers," he says. He stuffs the other bill and the wallet into your pocket.

"Now are you going to come with me to get an ice cream cone or shall I tell the clerk you took the money?" Jerry asks.

If you go with him, turn to page 49.

If you say "No!," turn to page 31.

40

You tell Jerry, "Look, Jerry, I can't take the money. I am going to return the wallet to Mr. French. Do you want to come with me?"

Jerry answers, "No way! If you return it, you do it yourself." Then he turns and runs off.

You look for a phone to call Mr. French. There is a pay phone on the corner by the gas station. You walk slowly toward it.

As you walk you think about what you will say. When you get there, you drop your coin in the phone and dial the phone number in the wallet.

The phone rings and rings. No one answers. You think maybe you should take the wallet home and phone again from there.

If you decide to go home and call, turn to page 53.

If you decide to let it ring longer, turn to page 43.

Phone
TIRES

Finally someone answers in a breathless voice, "Hello, this is Mr. French."

You give your name and say, "I am down at the gas station on Main Street. I found your wallet. What would you like me to do with it?"

"Stay where you are," replies Mr. French. "I will come right down and get it. I'll be there in less than five minutes."

He is there in three minutes. You hand him the wallet. "Thank you for calling me. It would have been easy for some people to borrow a little money," he says.

You blush, thinking of Jerry and how you almost did take money. Since he is waiting for an answer, you say, "Well, sir, I did think about it. But I decided it just wasn't right. I'll be going now."

"Goodbye, and thank you again for returning my wallet."

The End

44

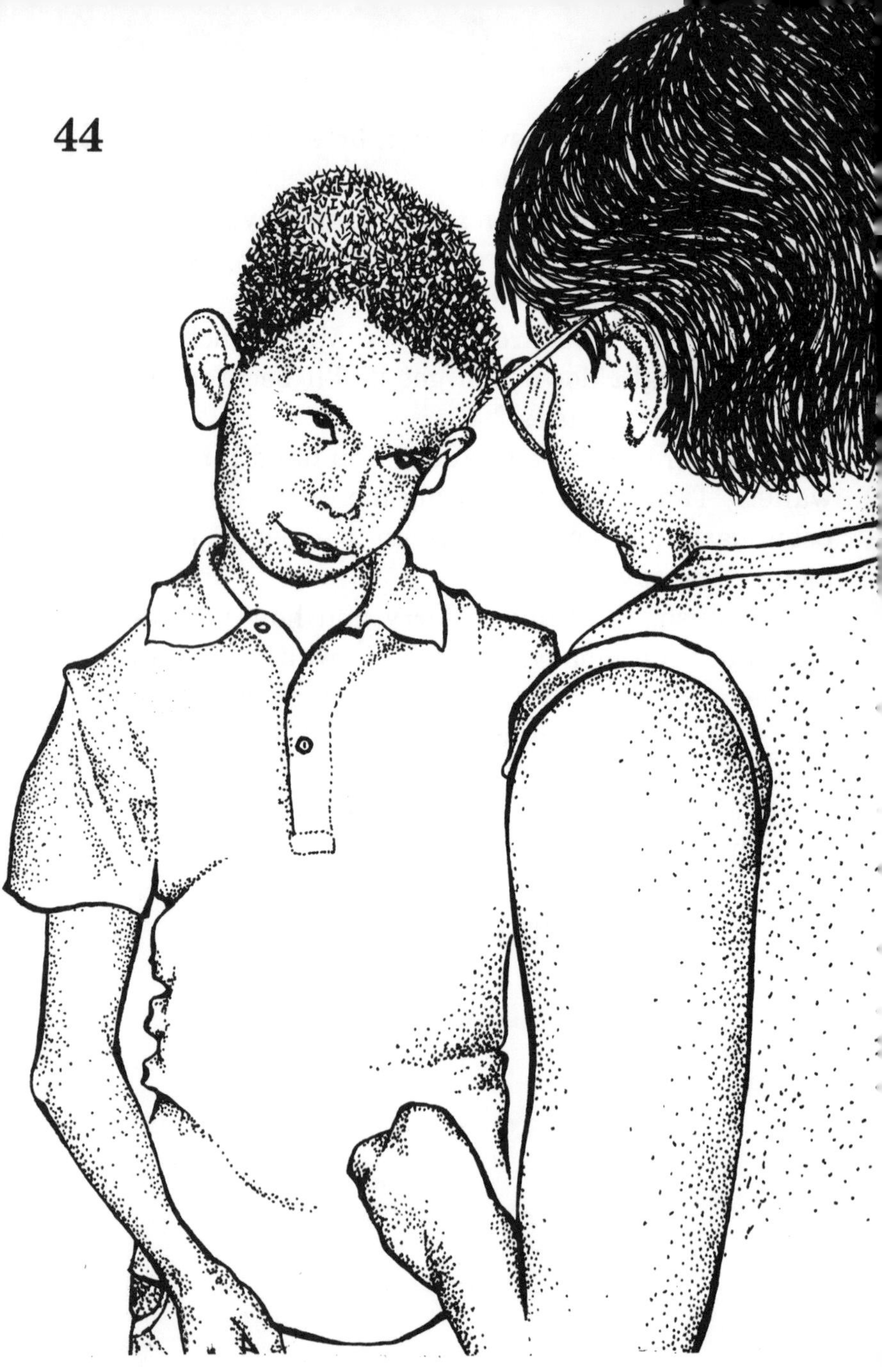

Jerry knows you are not sure. "Come on, Tyrone," he pleads, "he's not going to miss a measly two dollars."

You know Mr. French. He has lots of money and probably won't miss it, but you still don't think it is right.

"Come on," urges Jerry, "Imagine how good an ice cream cone would taste. What is your favorite flavor?"

If you decide he really would not miss the money and go for the cone, turn to page 47.

If you still can't decide, turn to page 34.

Your conscience bothers you a little, but not enough to stop you. It is so hot you really want an ice cream cone.

You and Jerry run to the ice cream shop. Jerry orders a Rocky Road cone and you order a strawberry.

As you leave the store, you ask Jerry, "What shall we do with the wallet now?"

"Drop it in the mailbox," he says. "Let them deliver it." You drop the wallet in the mailbox, then sit down beside Jerry.

While you eat, you think about how you would feel if someone took money from your wallet. Jerry says, "Isn't this great?"

You don't say anything. You're not sure it is great. It is true you didn't get caught (at least this time). But you did not enjoy the cone as much as you thought you would.

The End

48

You follow Jerry into the ice cream shop.

Jerry orders and then the clerk turns to you and asks, "What do you want, Tyrone?"

"A double scoop of strawberry on a sugar cone, please." You order and hand him the dollar.

As you put the change back into your pocket, Mr. French's wallet falls out.

"Uh oh," you say, and quickly pick up the wallet and put it back. But not quick enough.

"That's a pretty big wallet for a kid. Is it really yours, Tyrone?" the clerk asks.

You open your mouth but you can't think of anything to say.

"Let me see it," he says in a stern voice.

If you give it to him, turn to page 27.

If you say no and run out, turn to page 20.

"Not exactly," you reply reluctantly.

Your mother waits and then asks, "What does 'not exactly' mean?"

"Jerry took some money for an ice cream cone, but I didn't take any."

"Okay, I will dial the number for Mr. French. You can tell him that you have his wallet, and he can pick it up here at his convenience. I will explain what happened to the money," Mom says as she dials the phone.

Mr. French answers the phone and she hands it to you. "Hello, Mr. French, this is Tyrone. I found your wallet at the park today. You can pick it up at our house when you want to."

"Thank you for calling. I will be right over," he replies.

You give a sigh of relief. Your part is done.

The End

52 Before you tell Jerry what you have decided, he puts the money back in the wallet. Then he laid down beside the wallet to wait for your answer.

You bend down and grab the wallet. "I'm taking it back. Coming with me?"

"Oh, all right," Jerry replies, "but we could have had a delicious ice cream cone."

The two of you go to the pool clerk and say, "We found this wallet near the big tree out front. It belongs to Mr. French."

"Oh, good," the clerk replies, "you can give it to him right now. He's in the locker room hunting for it."

You enter the locker room and go up to the man looking under a bench. "Mr. French," you say as you hand him the wallet, "Jerry and I found your wallet outside."

"Well, thank you. I'm glad to get it back. What do you say to two dollars each for a reward?"

"That sounds fine to me," you and Jerry say together.

The End

You put the wallet into your pocket and head for home. As you walk, you think about what you will tell your mom.

You decide to tell her the whole truth. She will be disappointed you didn't leave the wallet at the pool. But you are pretty sure she won't be mad since you didn't use any of the money. You know she will know how to give it back.

Suddenly you feel a little better and run home. You burst in the back door and almost crash into your mom.

"Mom, when Jerry and I were at the park, we found a wallet. It belongs to Mr. French. I tried phoning him from the phone booth near the ice cream store, but he didn't answer."

"Is everything in the wallet just the way you found it?" your mother asks.

"Well..." you pause and look at your shoes. "If I tell the truth, Jerry will be mad at me. If I lie, Mom will be mad. How can I answer so neither Mom nor Jerry will be mad?"

If you decide to tell the simple truth, turn to page 50.

If you decide to hide the truth, turn to page 55.

54

"Errr ..." you think, "what can I say so I won't get in trouble and make Jerry mad?" Suddenly you have an idea.

"Well, *I* didn't take anything," you answer.

"Tyrone, I am glad you didn't take anything. Are you sure no one else took anything? Before you answer, remember Mr. French will probably know if some money or credit cards are missing."

"Jerry took a dollar for an ice cream cone."

"Thank you for telling me. I will phone, and when he comes I will explain the missing money."

Later Mr. French picks up the wallet. He thanks you for returning it and tells you that he will ask Jerry to replace the money he took. "But," Mr French adds, "I will tell him in a way that doesn't involve you. Thank you again for returning the wallet."

"Whew! I'm glad that is over," you think. "Next time anyone tempts me I think I'll say 'no,' and turn in the wallet as fast as I can," you promise yourself.

The End

56 You decide to give the wallet to Jerry. If he sees you try to give it to him he will probably refuse to take it. Somehow you have to hide the wallet.

You look around for an idea. Suddenly you see an old paper bag. You look around to check that no one else can see you. Then you take the wallet from your pocket and put it into the bag.

The next step is to give Jerry the bag. You think about what you will say. Before you can decide, the clock on the town hall chimes three. The chimes give you an idea and you walk into the ice cream shop.

"Jerry," you say, holding the bag behind you, "I can't wait any longer. I just remembered I promised my mom I would be home by three." Then you toss him the bag and say, "Here is your package."

Quickly you leave the shop and run home. When you get there, your mom says, "Tyrone, I'm so glad you are home. Uncle Willis called and invited you to go fishing. He will pick you up in fifteen minutes."

The End

You leave your name and phone number with the clerk.

That night after supper the phone rings. Your dad answers and talks for a bit.

When he hangs up the phone, he turns to you and says, "I am proud of you. A Mr. French called to thank you for returning his wallet. He said that all the money was still there. I'm pleased you didn't take any. It would have been easy for some people to take a little bit and hope it was not missed."

Then he gives you a hug!

The End